To Hope,
all my love

T.M.

BLOOMSBURY CHILDREN'S BOOKS
Bloomsbury Publishing Plc
50 Bedford Square, London WC1B 3DP, UK
29 Earlsfort Terrace, Dublin 2, Ireland

BLOOMSBURY, BLOOMSBURY CHILDREN'S BOOKS and the Diana logo
are trademarks of Bloomsbury Publishing Plc

First published in Great Britain in 2023 by Bloomsbury Publishing Plc

A catalogue record for this book is available from the British Library

ISBN 978 1 4088 9963 2 (HB)
ISBN 978 1 4088 9964 9 (PB)
ISBN 978 1 4088 9962 5 (eBook)

1 3 5 7 9 10 8 6 4 2

Printed and bound in China by Leo Paper Products, Heshan, Guangdong

MIX
Paper from
responsible sources
FSC® C020056
FSC
www.fsc.org

To find out more about our authors and books
visit www.bloomsbury.com and sign up for our newsletters

# More
# Peas
# Please!

Tom McLaughlin

BLOOMSBURY
CHILDREN'S BOOKS

LONDON  OXFORD  NEW YORK  NEW DELHI  SYDNEY

It all started on Tuesday
when **Milo** and his sister **Molly**
were eating supper . . .

Milo gobbled up his lasagne, then

# "FINISHED!"

he said,
jumping down
from the table.

"You **haven't** finished!" said Molly.
"What about your peas?
You haven't touched them!"

"I can't eat PEAS!"
exclaimed Milo.

"There are **LOTS** of things wrong with them!" said Milo.

"Why not?" asked Molly, "what's wrong with peas?"

"They're too **GREEN!**
Greener than a stinky, swampy pond,
greener than a giant dragon,

greener than a fleet of **space-sick aliens.** "

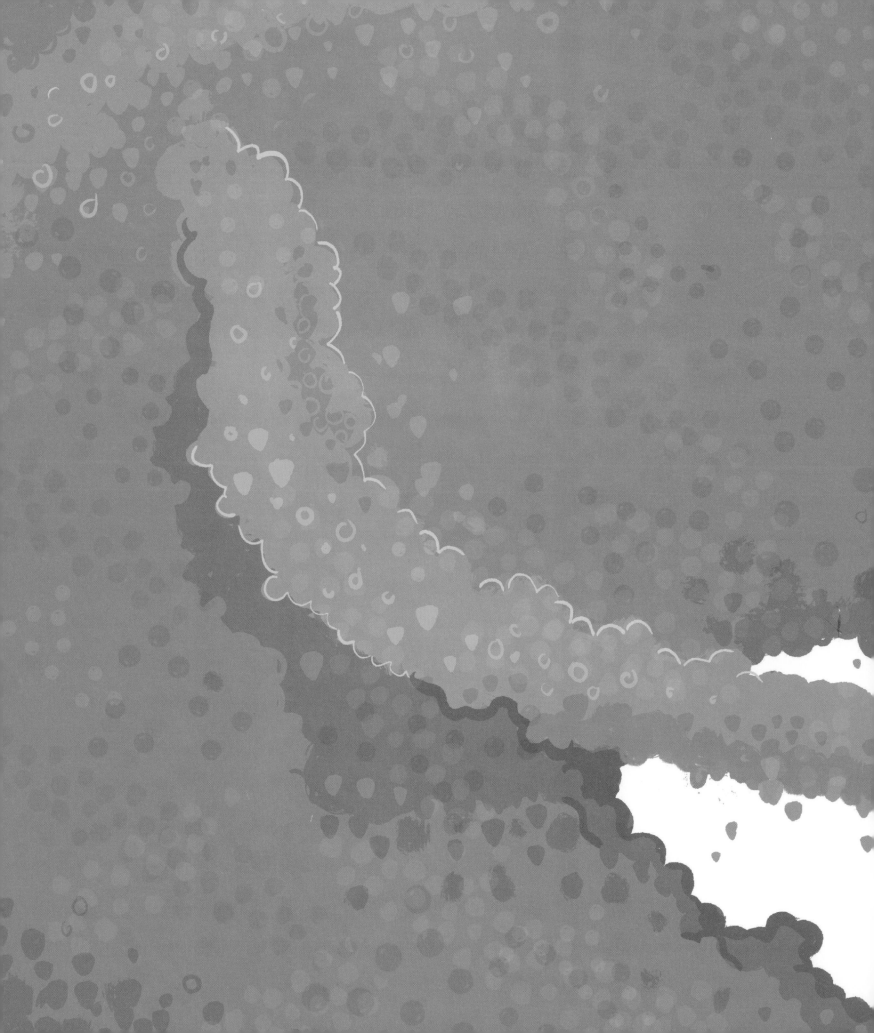

"And there are too many of them.

There's a whole **MOUNTAIN** of them.

And they're after me -

Help!"

"Don't be silly!" said Molly. "Peas are delicious.
They'll make you **super SUPER STRONG!**

Stronger than
a muscle man
lifting a digger,

stronger than
an elephant
pulling a tree,

stronger than
a **T. rex**
juggling planets."

"They'll make you **TALL!**

Taller than a skyscraper,

taller than Mount Everest,

taller than a ladder
reaching all the way
to the **moon**."

"And they'll make you **SMART**.
Smarter than a crafty fox,
smarter than a robot with TWO heads!

Don't you want to be **strong**
and **tall** and **smart?**" asked Molly.

Milo thought
for a bit. "Well—"

"Because I know I do!"

said Molly,

reaching for

Milo's plate.

"Hey!"
screamed Milo,
"those are
MINE!"

“Oh no!”

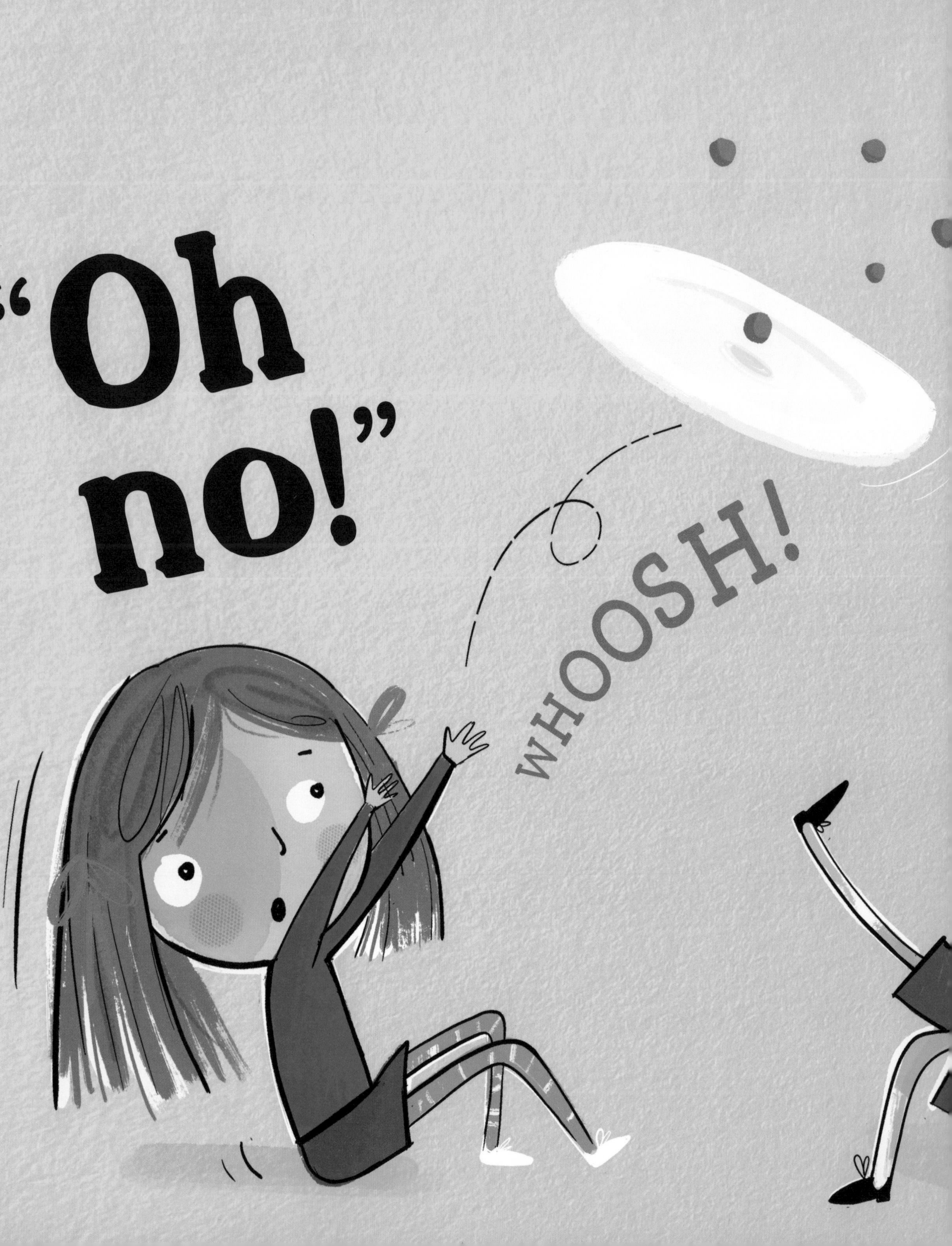

# PLEASE!"